W9-BOB-324

GILLY MARTIN THE FOX

RETOLD BY
MOLLIE HUNTER

ILLUSTRATED BY
DENNIS McDERMOTT

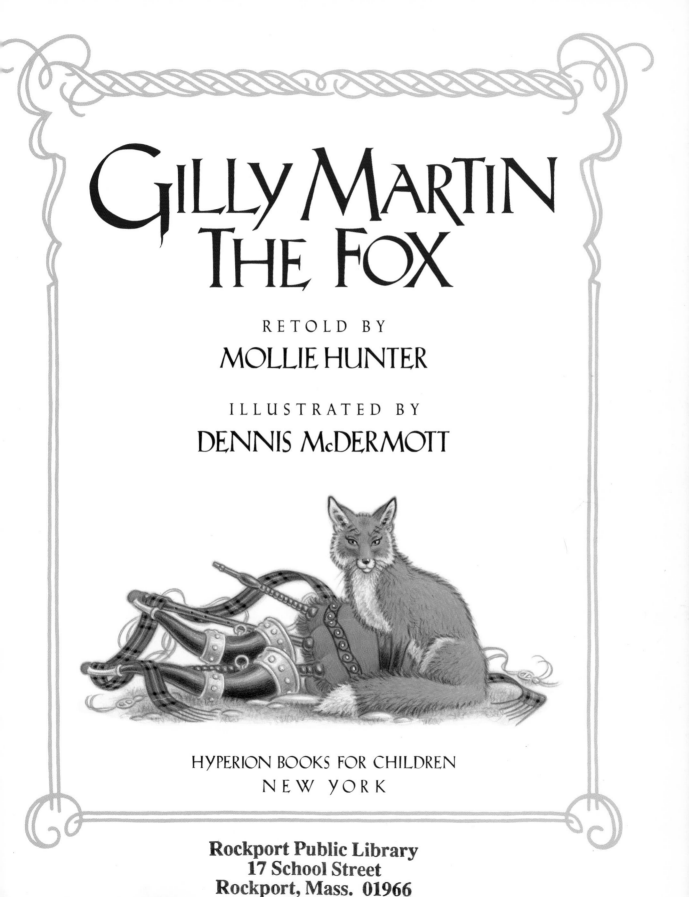

HYPERION BOOKS FOR CHILDREN
NEW YORK

AUTHOR'S NOTE

This story is a much-condensed but nevertheless faithful retelling of a many-centuries-old tale from the Scottish Highlands, as told in Gaelic to John Dewar by Angus Campbell, quarryman, Knock-derry, Roseneath, Scotland, and written down in the Gaelic by Dewar. Translated into English by John Francis Campbell, it was then published (by Edmonston & Douglas, Edinburgh, 1860) as "Mac Iain Direach" (Son of John the Upright) in Volume 2 of Campbell's collection, *Popular Tales of the West Highlands*.

Text © 1994 by Maureen Mollie Hunter McIlwraith.
Illustrations © 1994 by Dennis McDermott.
All rights reserved. Printed in Hong Kong.
For information address Hyperion Books for Children,
114 Fifth Avenue, New York, New York 10011.
FIRST EDITION
1 3 5 7 9 10 8 6 4 2

Library of Congress Cataloging-in-Publication Data

Hunter, Mollie.
Gilly Martin the Fox/Mollie Hunter; illustrated by Dennis McDermott.
p. cm.
Summary: With the help of a shape-shifting fox, the Prince of
Alban goes on a series of quests among such enemies as the Giant
with Five Heads and the Seven Big Women of Jura.
ISBN 1-56282-517-8 (trade) — ISBN 1-56282-518-6 (lib. bdg.)
[1. Fairy tales.] I. McDermott, Dennis, ill. II. Title.
PZ8.H915Gi 1994
[E] — dc20 93-24112 CIP AC

The cover illustration is prepared using oil paint.
The interior illustrations are prepared using watercolor and ink.

This book is set in 14-point Trajanus.

For Neal—the one and only!
With love,
M. H.

For wee Carissa,
red-hair'd Sarah,
and bonnie Laura Jean.
—D. McD.

Gilly Martin the Fox was going quietly about his own business one day, when who should he meet but the young Prince of Alban looking very sorry for himself!

Now there was nothing Gilly Martin liked better than poking his sharp nose into other people's affairs. Also, he had his own strange ways of solving problems, and all this made him instantly curious to know why such a rich and handsome young prince should be wandering all alone and looking so sad.

"Well now, Prince of Alban," said he, "what brings you here? And why are you so down in the mouth?"

"I am here," the prince told him, "because I am under a spell to search for a certain bird that has magical powers as a hunter of game. The Blue Falcon is its name, and it is the Witch of Alban who has me in her spell. She has no reason for this, either, except that she is the wickedest witch in the whole wide world. And I am down in the mouth because, even if I do find this bird for her, she still plans that I will die a terrible death."

"Then you *are* in a pickle!" exclaimed Gilly Martin. "But I can show you the way out of it—providing, of course, that you can first prove you are brave enough to take all the risks you will meet!"

"I shall certainly try my best to be brave," declared the prince.

"Then come with me to the castle of the Giant with Five Heads," said Gilly Martin, "because it is he who owns the Blue Falcon. But I can tell you how to get it from him!"

Off they went together then, with Gilly Martin explaining as they went how the prince could get the Blue Falcon from the giant.

"But take care!" he warned also. "When you are running away with the falcon, you must not let so much as a feather of hers touch anything inside the giant's castle, or it will go badly for you!"

"I will take care," promised the prince, and strode quickly up to knock at the door of the castle. A great roaring voice came from within.

"Who knocks at my door?"

"A strong young man seeking work," shouted the prince.

"And what kind of work can you do?"

"I can herd cows, sheep, and goats. And you never saw anyone so good as I am at taking care of hens and ducks."

Once again came the great roaring voice. "That is just the kind of servant I want."

The door of the castle opened, and out came a horrible five-headed giant. But the prince was indeed as brave as he was handsome, and so he boldly faced up to this monster.

He was as good as his word, too, when it came to taking care of all the giant's livestock, and he worked so hard at this—but especially at looking after the hens and ducks—that the giant began to say to himself, "This is a good lad, and he really does know how to take care of birds. I think there might come a day when I even allow him to look after my Blue Falcon!"

That day came at last, and the prince said to himself, "Now is my chance!"

He seized hold of the Blue Falcon and began to creep out of the castle. But when the falcon saw daylight outside the castle door, it opened its wings to spring into the air. The tip of one wing touched the doorpost, the doorpost let out a screech, and the giant came running.

"Aha!" he roared, snatching the Blue Falcon from the prince. "You will not get *that* from me! Not unless I get something I want even more in exchange for it!"

"And what is that?" asked the prince.

"A sword!" roared the giant. "The only one that can defeat every foe! The magic sword they call the White Glave of Light!"

"We must go to the island of Jura," said Gilly Martin once the prince had told him of all this, "because it is the Seven Big Women of Jura who own the White Glave of Light. But I can tell you how to get it from them."

Off they went together, then, until they saw the island of Jura rising out of the sea in front of them. And as they went, Gilly Martin told the prince what he must do there.

"But remember," he warned again, "when you are running away with the magic sword you must not let the sheath of it touch anything inside the house of the Seven Big Women, or things will go badly for you."

"I will remember," promised the prince, and began looking around for a boat so that he could row himself across to Jura.

Gilly Martin smiled to see this, his own cunning Gilly Martin smile. Because he was what they call a shape shifter—which means that he could change himself into any shape that he liked.

Straightaway, then—to the great astonishment of the prince—Gilly changed himself into a sturdy little rowboat. The prince stepped gladly into this, rowed himself over to Jura, and once there, he did as Gilly Martin had told him.

He knocked at the door of the house of the Seven Big Women and offered to work for them at polishing everything they had of gold, silver, iron, or steel.

Now the Seven Big Women were lazy creatures. Besides which, the prince spoke so politely to them and smiled so pleasantly that straightaway they agreed: "Yes, we would be happy to have a young man like you for that kind of work."

"And I," said the prince gallantly, "will be very happy to work for you."

He set to it with a will then, polishing everything made of metal until it was so clear and bright that the Seven Big Women said, "This is the best servant lad we have ever had. There might even come a day when we let him polish the White Glave of Light!"

That day came at last, and the prince took such care of the magic sword and polished it so brightly that the Seven Big Women were content to be away from home one day and leave him alone with it.

"Now is my chance!" he told himself. He ran to the door, carrying the great length of the sword over his shoulder. But just as he passed through the door, the tip of the sword's sheath touched the lintel, the lintel let out a screech, and the Seven Big Women came running.

"Aha!" they chorused, snatching the sword from him. "You will not get *that* from us! Not unless we get something we want even more in exchange for it."

"And what is that?" asked the prince.

"A horse! The Bay Filly that belongs to the King of Erin!" With one voice, the Seven Big Women shouted their desire. And sadly, once more, the prince went off to look for Gilly Martin.

"Well now," said Gilly Martin when he heard this tale, "the Bay Filly is greatly treasured by the King of Erin because there is a magic on her that means she can run faster than any wind. But I can tell you how to get her from him."

The prince listened again to what Gilly Martin had to tell him. And again, Gilly Martin finished with a warning.

"But remember," he said, "when you are taking away the Bay Filly you must not let any part of her except her hooves touch anything inside her stable, or things will go badly for you."

"I will remember," promised the prince. And so Gilly Martin changed his shape again—turning himself this time into a sailing ship that took the prince over the sea to the land of Erin.

Quickly he leapt ashore there and hurried to speak to the gatekeeper of the king's palace. The gatekeeper called to the king that there was a strong young man seeking work, and the king said, "What kind of work can you do?"

"I can feed and groom horses," the prince told him. "I can clean the silver and steel and leather of their harness, and keep all in the best order that even a king would want."

"Then you are just the kind of servant for me!" exclaimed the king, and straightaway he ordered the prince to be put to work in his stables.

The king was well pleased then, because his new servant took such great care of all his horses. And as for the Bay Filly, the prince fed and groomed her so well that her coat had never been so sleek nor her harness so shiny.

"This is a good stable lad," said the king. "Such a good one, indeed, that I see I may put the Bay Filly entirely in his care."

Away he went then on a day's hunting, and the prince said to himself, "Now is my chance!"

He laid hold of the Bay Filly and began to lead her out of her stable. But when he was taking her through the stable door, she gave a swish of her tail. The tip of her tail touched the side of the door, the door gave out a screech, and the king came running.

"Aha!" shouted he, snatching the Bay Filly's reins from the prince. "You will not get *that* from me. Not unless you give me something I want even more in exchange."

"And what is that?" asked the prince.

"A wife!" cried the king. "The beautiful daughter of the King of Lochlann to be my queen!"

"It is over the sea to the land of Lochlann we must go, then," said Gilly Martin when the prince came back to him with this latest tale. "But you have not so far done exactly what I told you, and so, after you have let the King of Lochlann hear the story I have prepared for you, you must leave everything to me."

"I will," agreed the prince—who was beginning by then to despair of anything going right for him. He listened carefully then to

the story he was supposed to tell the King of Lochlann; and once this story was finished, Gilly Martin again changed himself into a sailing ship—this time, a large beautiful one.

The ship went swiftly, easily sailing—but when it reached Lochlann, it drove wildly ashore and stuck there! The prince leapt down from it and hurried to the palace of the king.

"I am the Prince of Alban," he announced there.

Much impressed by this, the palace guards took him straight to see the king. Sadly then, he told the story of storm and shipwreck that Gilly Martin had invented for him, and the king was sorry to hear this.

"We must see what we can do to help you," he decided. And so he and his queen and their beautiful daughter, the Princess of Lochlann, all went with the prince to look at his ship.

It was lying aground, just as he had told them. But now there was a sound of strange but very sweet music coming from it, and this made the princess very curious.

"I should like to see the instrument that makes such music," said she.

"Then come aboard," invited the prince. And gladly, she agreed to this.

From one part of the ship to another she ran, hoping always to find the instrument. But all the time she ran, the ship was backing away from the land and sailing farther and farther out to sea.

"Oh, oh!" cried she, seeing at last what had happened. "This is a bad trick you have played on me! Where are you taking me, Prince of Alban?"

"I am taking you to Erin," said the prince, "to give you as wife to the King of Erin so that I may get from him his Bay Filly to give to the Seven Big Women of Jura so that I may get from them the White Glave of Light to give to the Giant with Five Heads so that I may get from him the Blue Falcon to give to the Witch of Alban, who has me under her spell and who will yet be the cause of my death."

His face as he told this story was very sad—as well it might be because, from the moment he had first seen the beautiful Princess of Lochlann, he had felt himself falling in love with her. And softly then, he added, "But I would rather, much rather, be taking you as wife to myself."

The princess blushed like a rose at this because, from the moment she had first seen this handsome young prince, she had felt herself falling in love with him.

"I would rather that, too," said she shyly. And it was with this thought in both their minds that they sailed on to Erin.

The prince and princess went ashore on the land of Erin. And as soon as they had done so, Gilly Martin changed his shape from that of the ship to that of the princess.

"If it's a wife the King of Erin wants," he explained to the other two, "I'll give him 'wife'!"

Side by side, then, he and the prince set off for the king's palace—but not before the prince and princess had taken tender leave of one another, and she had anxiously cried after them: "I wish you well, my prince!"

The king got word that the Princess of Lochlann was being brought to him.

"Saddle the Bay Filly with a saddle of gold," he ordered, "and put a silver bridle on her."

The Bay Filly was saddled and bridled just as he had commanded. The king hurried out of the palace gate with her, all smiles at the sight of what he *thought* was the beautiful Princess of Lochlann. And smiling still, he gave the prince his Bay Filly.

But little did he guess it was Gilly Martin he had got in exchange. And sorry he was the moment he tried to embrace his new bride— because it was then that Gilly Martin changed back into his real shape.

"A fox!" cried the king. And a fox it was indeed that sprang upon him and chased and worried him, drawing such blood with its sharp teeth that he was the most thankful man alive when he finally saw the back of it.

As for Gilly Martin, he was smiling all over his face when he came back to tell the prince and the princess about the success of his trick. But there was still the matter of the Seven Big Women of Jura to be dealt with, and so he lost no time in changing himself into a ship big enough to take both prince and princess—and, of course, the Bay Filly—to the island of Jura.

The ship reached Jura, and as soon as its passengers had gone ashore, Gilly Martin changed to his own shape for just long enough to explain to the prince and princess, "If it's riding the Seven Big Women want, I'll give them 'riding'!" And instantly then, he changed himself into the shape of the Bay Filly.

The prince handed the real Bay Filly into the care of the princess. Then away he went with the false Bay Filly—but not before he and the princess had again taken tender leave of one another and she had again told him: "I wish you well! Oh, I *do* wish you well!"

The Seven Big Women of Jura saw him coming with what they *thought* was the Bay Filly. And seizing the White Glave of Light, they rushed out to meet him.

The prince handed over the filly in exchange for the glave. He hurried off with it, leaving the Seven Big Women in such haste to ride the Bay Filly that his back was hardly turned before the first one was up on her.

Another one mounted behind her, then another, and another, with Gilly Martin always stretching his back and stretching it again until there was room for all seven of them to be seated on it. Then away he raced—and if the March wind could run fast, he could run faster!

Over the moors and up and down the mountains of Jura he sped. Right to the top of the highest mountain on the island he galloped and charged to the very edge of its highest cliff. He dug in hard with his forefeet there, then up went his hind end—and over the edge went tumbling every one of the Seven Big Women!

Laughing all over his face then, Gilly Martin changed back to his own shape and ran to where the prince and princess and the Bay Filly were waiting for him.

"Now to deal with the Giant with Five Heads!" said he. And once more, he turned himself into a ship.

The ship reached the prince's own land of Alban. And when the prince and princess and the Bay Filly had gone ashore there, Gilly Martin became himself again for just the moment it took to explain to the other two, "If it's a battle that's wanted by the Giant with Five Heads, I'll give him 'battle'!"

Again on the instant then, he changed himself into the White Glave of Light. The prince gave the Bay Filly and the real glave into the care of the princess. Then off he went with the false glave—but not before he and the princess had taken a third and even more tender farewell of one another.

The Giant with Five Heads saw him coming toward the castle and rushed out carrying the Blue Falcon. Eagerly he took from the prince what he *thought* was the White Glave of Light and handed over the falcon in exchange.

Roaring with glee then, he began swinging the glave wildly around his five heads and boasting of all the mighty battles he meant to fight with it. But it was not long that he boasted, and no battles did he fight!

At the very height of all this playacting, Gilly Martin bent himself into a curve that made the glave curl back toward the giant, instead of swinging away from him. And at one stroke, this big, sharp curve of steel cut off every one of the giant's five heads.

Back into his own shape went Gilly Martin, leaping over the five heads and laughing out loud over what he had done. Quickly then, he returned to where the prince and princess were waiting for him. They were embracing very fondly by that time, he found, and they were both eager to tell him how much they longed to be married to one another.

"Yet how can we marry," lamented the prince, "when the Witch of Alban is so determined that I shall die?"

"Ah!" said Gilly Martin. "But that need not happen, Prince— not if you have the courage to do as I tell you now."

"I have the courage to do *anything* that will win me the princess," cried the prince. "And so speak on, Gilly Martin. Speak on."

Gilly Martin spoke. And for once the Prince of Alban then did exactly what he was told to do. He rode the Bay Filly back to his own home in Alban with the princess mounted behind him, the Blue Falcon on his wrist, and the White Glave of Light by his side.

Gilly Martin trotted alongside the Bay Filly, and outside of the prince's home, they found the Witch of Alban waiting to shoot at him a glance so full of evil that it would bring him to a terrible death. But the prince knew exactly what he meant to do about that!

He charged toward the witch with the White Glave of Light held up so that the flat of its broad blade was between him and that deadly glance. Then, at the last second of his charge, he turned the edge of the blade toward her. And down she went before the

magic in that sharp and glittering edge—no longer a witch but
just a heap of rotten old firewood!

The prince leapt down from the Bay Filly. He set fire to all that
was left of the witch, and so at last he was free from all her spells.
Besides which, he had got the princess for his wife, the Blue Falcon
to keep him always supplied with game, the Bay Filly to let him
ride swifter than the wind, and the White Glave of Light to defeat
every foe.

"And so let this be my reward to you!" he cried to Gilly Martin. "You shall go freely through all my lands, you and all of your kin. And forever and always, the law of Alban shall be that none of you shall ever come to any harm."

Gilly Martin smiled at this, his own cunning Gilly Martin smile. "You can make good that promise to every other fox in this land," said he, "but *I* have no need of it—because I am Gilly Martin the shape shifter, and so I am well able to take care of myself."

Away he went then to carry on attending to his own business— but also, of course, to continue poking his nose into other people's affairs. And that, by all accounts, is what he is still doing to this very day.